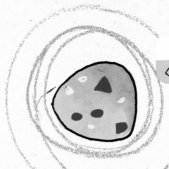

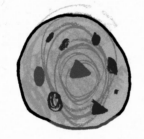
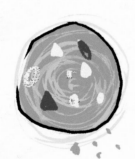

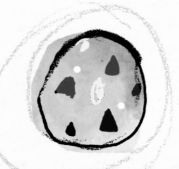

In memory of my mum—J.R.
For Dan x— C.E.

little bee books

An imprint of Bonnier Publishing Group
853 Broadway, New York, NY 10003
Copyright © 2014 by Jamie Rix
Illustrations copyright © 2014 by Clare Elsom
First published in Great Britain by Piccadilly Press.
This little bee books edition, 2015.
All rights reserved, including the right of reproduction in whole or in part in any form.
LITTLE BEE BOOKS is a trademark of Bonnier Publishing Group,
and associated colophon is a trademark of Bonnier Publishing Group.
Manufactured in China 0415024
First Edition 2 4 6 8 10 9 7 5 3 1
Library of Congress Control Number: 2014958643
ISBN 978-1-4998-0086-9

www.littlebeebooks.com
www.bonnierpublishing.com

# The Last Chocolate Chip Cookie

by
## Jamie Rix

Illustrated by
## Clare Elsom

little bee books

There was one chocolate chip cookie left on the plate, so I leaned across the table and took it.

"Jack," gasped my mom. "Where are your manners? Offer the last chocolate chip cookie to everyone else first."

"Everyone else?" I asked.

"Everyone else," she insisted.

So I put the last chocolate chip cookie
in my pocket and did as I was told.

I offered it
to my brother,
but he didn't want it.

I offered it to my dad, but he didn't want it.

I offered it to Gran,

and even to the cat,

but they didn't want it.

So I offered the last chocolate chip cookie to my teacher,

the window cleaner,

the bus driver,

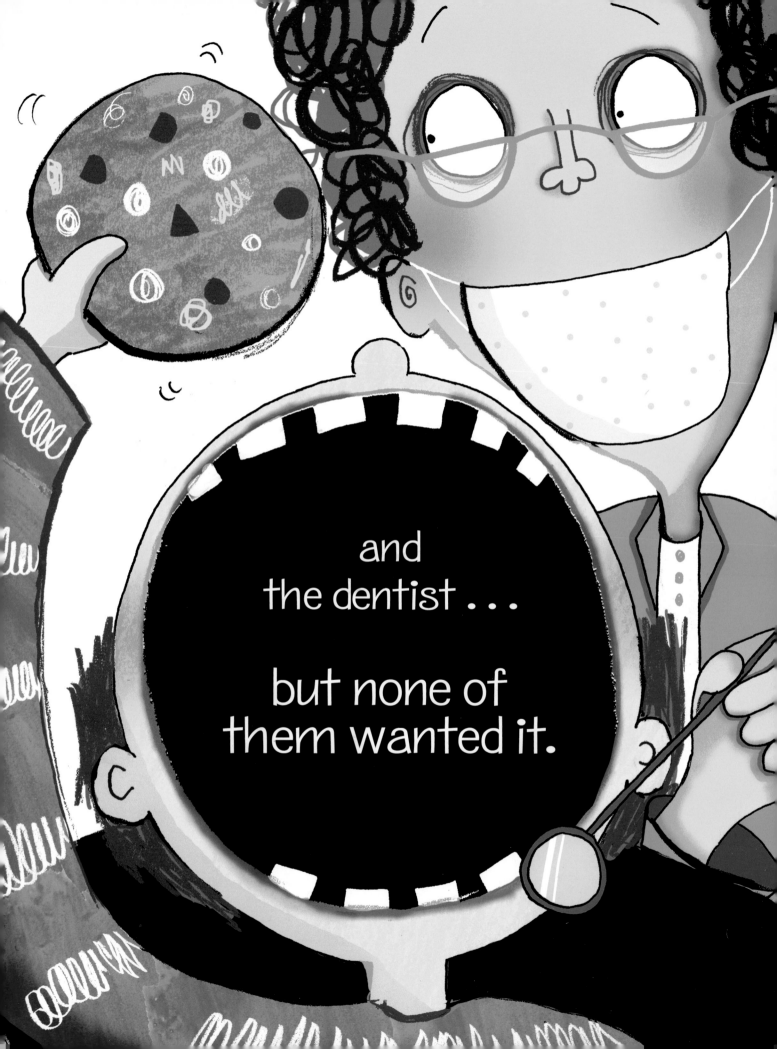

I went all around the world and offered
it to anyone I could find, including
a Mexican baker with a mustache.

But no one wanted it.

So I took the last chocolate chip cookie
into space and offered
it to an alien.

But the alien didn't want to eat
the last chocolate chip cookie . . .

He wanted to eat ME!

"Splagly!" gasped his mom.
"Where are your manners?
Offer the human being to everyone else first."

"EVERYONE else?" he asked.

"EVERYONE else," she insisted.

So Splagly put me in his pocket and did as he was told.

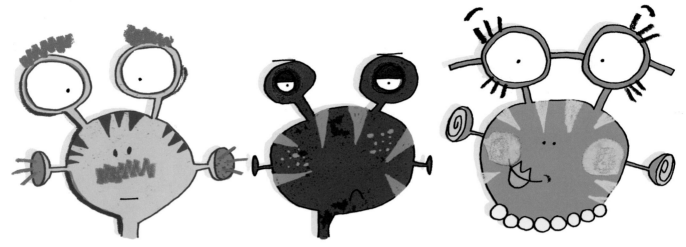

He offered me to his daddle, his brotter, his grin-gran,

the cattamog, his wormhole teacher, the spaceship cleaner,

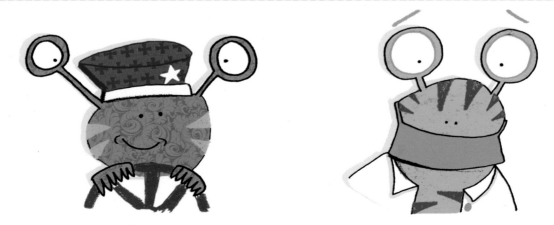

the spacebus pilot, and the fang-filler.

He flew all around the universe and
offered me to any alien he could find . . .
including a four-eyed
Bogly Marsh-masher.

But no one wanted me . . .

... until he arrived back on Earth

and
offered
me to
my mom.

"Yes, I would like him, please," she said.
"It's lovely to meet an alien with such good manners."

I told my mom that I offered the last chocolate chip cookie to everyone else, but nobody wanted it.

"Then you can eat it," she said.
"It will taste twice as delicious now
that you've been so polite."

As I took it out of my pocket, I was drooling.

I'd waited a long time to eat the last chocolate chip cookie.

I took a bite . . .

# IT TASTED LIKE CARDBOARD GUNK-GLOOP WITH HAIRS ON IT!

Do YOU want the last chocolate chip cookie?

# LAST CHOCOLATE CHIP COOKIE RECIPE:

## YOU NEED:

3/4 cup of butter

1 cup and 2 tablespoons of superfine granulated sugar

2 eggs

2 3/4 cups self-rising flour

2/3 cup of chocolate chips

**ALSO:**
**LARGE BAKING TRAY**
**MIXING BOWL**
**ELECTRIC MIXER**

## GET COOKING: *

Preheat oven to 360°F

Add all ingredients to bowl and mix well

Spoon dollops of the mixture onto baking tray

(grease the tray first and leave lots of room between dollops)

Bake in oven for 15-20 minutes until golden

**EAT, ENJOY, AND DON'T LEAVE THEM IN YOUR POCKET TILL THEY'RE MOLDY!**

**\* get an adult to help with the oven!**